THE INSIDE-OUTSIDE
BOOK OF PARIS

ROXIE MUNRO

DUTTON CHILDREN'S BOOKS   NEW YORK

Published in the United States by Dutton Children's Books,
a division of Penguin Books USA Inc.
375 Hudson Street, New York, New York 10014

Designer: Joseph Rutt

Printed in Hong Kong by South China Printing Co.
First Edition   10 9 8 7 6 5 4 3 2 1

Library of Congress Cataloging-in-Publication Data

Munro, Roxie.
    The inside-outside book of Paris/by Roxie Munro.—1st ed.
        p. cm.
    Summary: Captioned illustrations depict noted sights in Paris, including
the Eiffel Tower, the Arch of Triumph, the Metro subway, and a puppet
theater. A section of text provides information on each sight.
    ISBN 0-525-44863-2
    1. Paris (France)—Description—Views—Juvenile literature.
[1. Paris (France)—Pictorial works.] I. Title.
DC707.M896   1992
944′.361′00222—dc20   91-29318 CIP AC

To Bo, because it's Paris

Acknowledgments
Thanks to Donna Brooks, my editor; Bo Zaunders, for his
help with research; Karen Lotz; Joseph Rutt, for book
design; and in Paris, JoAnne Morning.

Musée d'Orsay

The enormous vaulted space of the Orsay Museum was originally a railroad station. Built of glass and steel in 1900, it has now been turned into one of the most popular museums in Paris, specializing in nineteenth-century art. Over six hundred people work inside, greeting visitors and taking care of the vast exhibits. Spanning the years 1848 to 1914, the Orsay collections feature many Impressionist paintings, as well as sculpture, decorative arts, photography, and the very earliest films.

Looking through one of the old railroad clocks, visitors can gaze across the Seine, the river that winds through Paris, to the Tuileries Gardens and, on the right, a former palace of many French kings, now a great museum—the Louvre. During the height of the tourist season, more than thirty thousand people a day may visit the Orsay Museum.

Booksellers along the Seine

Most days, depending upon the weather, sellers of old prints, maps, postcards, and secondhand books do a brisk business from their zinc-topped book boxes along both banks of the Seine. Here, browsers

enjoy the wares of a group of Left Bank booksellers, called
bouquinistes. In the background are the Pont St. Michel (a bridge)
and buildings on the Ile de la Cité (an island in the Seine).

Nearby is Shakespeare and Company, a bookstore started in the
1920s by Sylvia Beach. Originally located on Rue de l'Odéon, it
was a favorite haunt of writers like James Joyce, F. Scott Fitzgerald,
and Ernest Hemingway, who said he found books there that he had

never seen before. Now Shakespeare and Company has the largest
selection of English-language books on the continent of Europe.
On Sunday afternoons, book lovers can have tea and listen to
visiting authors talk about their books.

Jardin des Tuileries

Filled with statues of horses, nymphs, and gods, the Tuileries is a perfect example of a French formal garden. It was created in 1664, on the site of a tile-works factory that left behind its French name, *tuileries*. Adjoining the section shown here is a vast expanse of trees planted in an orderly pattern. In 1783, one of the first hot-air balloons was launched here.

This lavishly decorated merry-go-round under the trees, called *La Belle Epoque Carrousel*, gives rides to children for a few francs. Its name, meaning "The Good Old Days," refers to a period of elegance and gaiety that characterized Parisian life from the mid-nineteenth century until World War I.

L'Arc de Triomphe

A small plane once flew through this majestic arch, built by Napoléon in the early 1800s to commemorate his army's victories. The Arch of Triumph, 164 feet high and 148 feet wide, stands imposingly at Place Charles de Gaulle, where twelve avenues converge. Beneath the arch, an eternal flame marks the resting place of France's unknown soldier.

The view from the observation deck shows why the arch's location was originally called Place de l'Etoile (*étoile* means "star" in French). To the left, you can see the Champs-Elysées, the most famous avenue in Paris. Originally swampland, then a tree-lined promenade for carriages, it now draws throngs of tourists to its many cafés, shops, and theaters.

Ecole des Beaux-Arts

Once a residence for monks and later a museum, the Ecole des Beaux-Arts was established in 1816 as an art school. Students share studio space but work independently, meeting privately with their professors for instruction and critique. The school is located in the Latin Quarter, home of the Sorbonne, a university founded in 1215, when the language in all places of learning was Latin.

Café la Palette, down the street from the Ecole des Beaux-Arts, is a favorite hangout for artists. Paris has over twelve thousand cafés—gathering places where people can drink coffee and gossip, exchange ideas, read, or just watch the world go by. Cafés have been an integral part of the city's cultural and social life for over three hundred years.

Le Métro

The Metro (short for ''Metropolitan'') is the Paris subway system.
The Louvre station at Rue de Rivoli, one of several stops offering
riders a permanent art exhibition, is decorated with objects from the

grand museum above. Originally a medieval fortress, later a palace
added to and rebuilt many times, the Louvre is now one of the largest
art museums in the world. Topping a concourse under the courtyard
is a glass pyramid entrance designed by the American architect I. M. Pei.

The mural in the Bastille subway station commemorates the start of
the French Revolution, when mobs stormed the Bastille, a prison and
hated symbol of royal tyranny. The style of the subway entrance is

art nouveau, in vogue in 1900, when the first line opened for the Paris World Fair. One billion people a year now ride the attractive, clean, and—because of rubber wheels—quiet Paris subway.

Centre National d'Art Contemporain Georges Pompidou

Constructed in 1977, the bold, high-tech Pompidou Center contains collections of modern art and industrial design, as well as language labs, a bookstore, and even a children's museum. The center is also known as the Beaubourg, after the plateau on which it stands. On one side, the building's network of exposed pipes, ducts, and other fixtures reveal their functions through brightly painted colors: green for the water system, yellow for electrical circuits, blue for air-conditioning, and red for escalators and elevators.

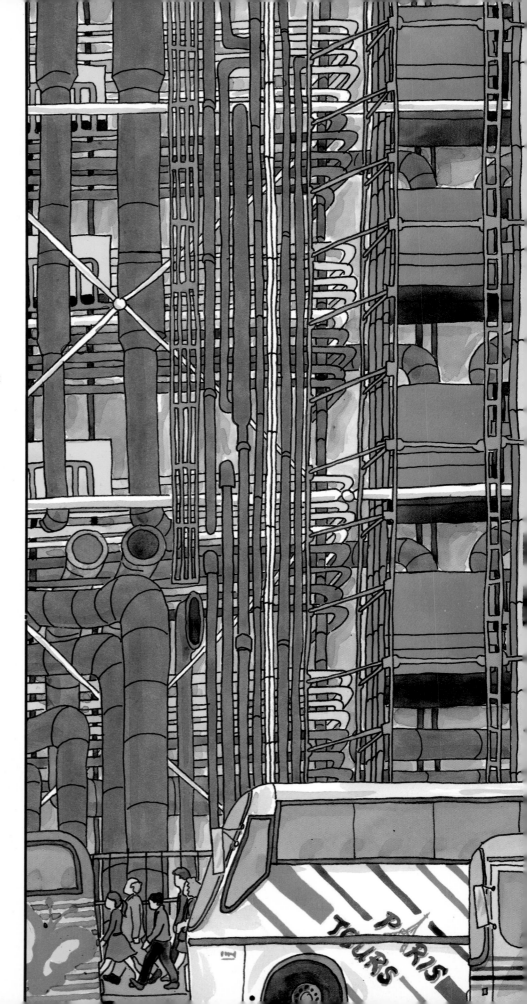

On the opposite side of the building, dizzying, see-through escalators offer a view across Paris all the way to Montmartre and the Basilica of the Sacred Heart, as well as a glimpse down to the street musicians, singers, and magicians performing in the square below.

Les Bateaux Mouches

The *bateaux mouches* (''river steamers'') travel under more than two dozen of the thirty-two bridges that cross the Seine in Paris. Originally these wide, flat boats offered Parisians cheap, convenient

transport, but now they primarily provide visitors with a leisurely
open-air tour of the city.

The bridges of Paris are low because river traffic consists mainly of barges. This single-span bridge, the ornate Pont Alexandre III, built in 1900, is only twenty-five feet above the water. Many of

the old barges tied up along the quays have been converted to floating homes.

Le Marché

Delicious fresh vegetables and fruits, poultry, fish, cheese, eggs, and butter are just some of the reasons to visit an open-air market, or *marché*. This one on the Rue Mouffetard tempts Parisians, who like to buy their food fresh each day, with everything from live chickens to cherries. Throughout Paris there are special markets for things like flowers, birds, or stamps, and there are also many flea and antique markets.

Shoppers may take home fresh baguettes of bread from the bakery, or *boulangerie*, as often as three times a day. This woman is going to her home in the Marais, one of the oldest districts of Paris, splendidly restored in recent times. Its twisting streets contain fine examples of seventeenth- and eighteenth-century mansions.

La Pâtisserie

In the sixteenth century, pastry making became an art in France.
By the seventeenth century, every city had its own pastry coat
of arms. The kitchen of this modern-day pastry shop, owned by

Monsieur Christian Pottier, employs six full-time pastry makers.
Every morning they turn out about eight hundred pure butter croissants,
followed by other luscious cakes and pastries throughout the day.

Appearance is just as important as taste where pastry is concerned.
Six basic doughs, whose recipes were developed centuries ago,
are the basis for all French pastries. Decorating with fruits, nuts,

chocolates, and glazes is an art in itself. One French pastry chef of
the early 1800s sought inspiration from museums and then made
etchings that were copied in pastry.

Marionnettes

Inside a small wooden building under the shade of trees in the Champs-de-Mars, the park next to the Eiffel Tower, is a puppet theater. It gives performances every Wednesday, Saturday, and Sunday, as well as on school holidays. Puppet shows are a favorite pastime of Parisian children. There are several other such theaters in Paris, including those in the Luxembourg Gardens and the Tuileries.

The beautifully costumed puppets (*marionnettes* in French) are made and operated by Luigi Tirelli, for whom being a puppeteer is a family tradition. These characters, from the French children's classic "Le Trézor du Roy d'Agobert," are constructed of wood, fabric, paint, and various decorative materials. Monsieur Tirelli also performs "Cinderella" and other well-known children's stories.

Tour Eiffel (jacket)

Called Gustave Eiffel's folly and "useless and monstrous" as it was being built, the Eiffel Tower is now without doubt the symbol of Paris. Erected for the 1889 Paris Universal Exposition, the tower was never meant to be permanent. But because the first transatlantic wireless telephones were operated from the tower, it endured. Composed of twelve thousand iron girders and two and a half million rivets, this 1,051-foot-high (including the antenna) structure took three hundred steeplejacks two years to build. Elevators and staircases go diagonally up the "legs." Bicyclists have ridden up the 1,792 steps, and an elephant once walked up them. In good weather, the view from the top extends forty-five to fifty miles.

Cathédrale de Notre-Dame de Paris (opening pages)

The Cathedral of Our Lady of Paris stands on the Ile de la Cité, a small island in the Seine where Celtic fishermen called Parisii settled around 250 B.C. Houses of worship have occupied the site for over two thousand years. The cathedral, a perfect example of Gothic architecture, was begun in 1193 and took 182 years to build. In medieval times, the finely chiseled stone figures on the three portal facades were intended to provide a sort of sculptural Bible for the common folk who couldn't read. All distances from Paris are measured from Kilomètre Zéro—a brass compasslike star embedded in the pavement outside the west door. From the tower, visitors can look northeast to see part of the Ile de la Cité, the River Seine, bridges, and embankments.

Fini